William Henderson, Charles Lyall

Who Wrote Shakespeare?

Aye, there's the rub

William Henderson, Charles Lyall

Who Wrote Shakespeare?
Aye, there's the rub

ISBN/EAN: 9783337222154

Printed in Europe, USA, Canada, Australia, Japan

Cover: Foto ©Andreas Hilbeck / pixelio.de

More available books at **www.hansebooks.com**

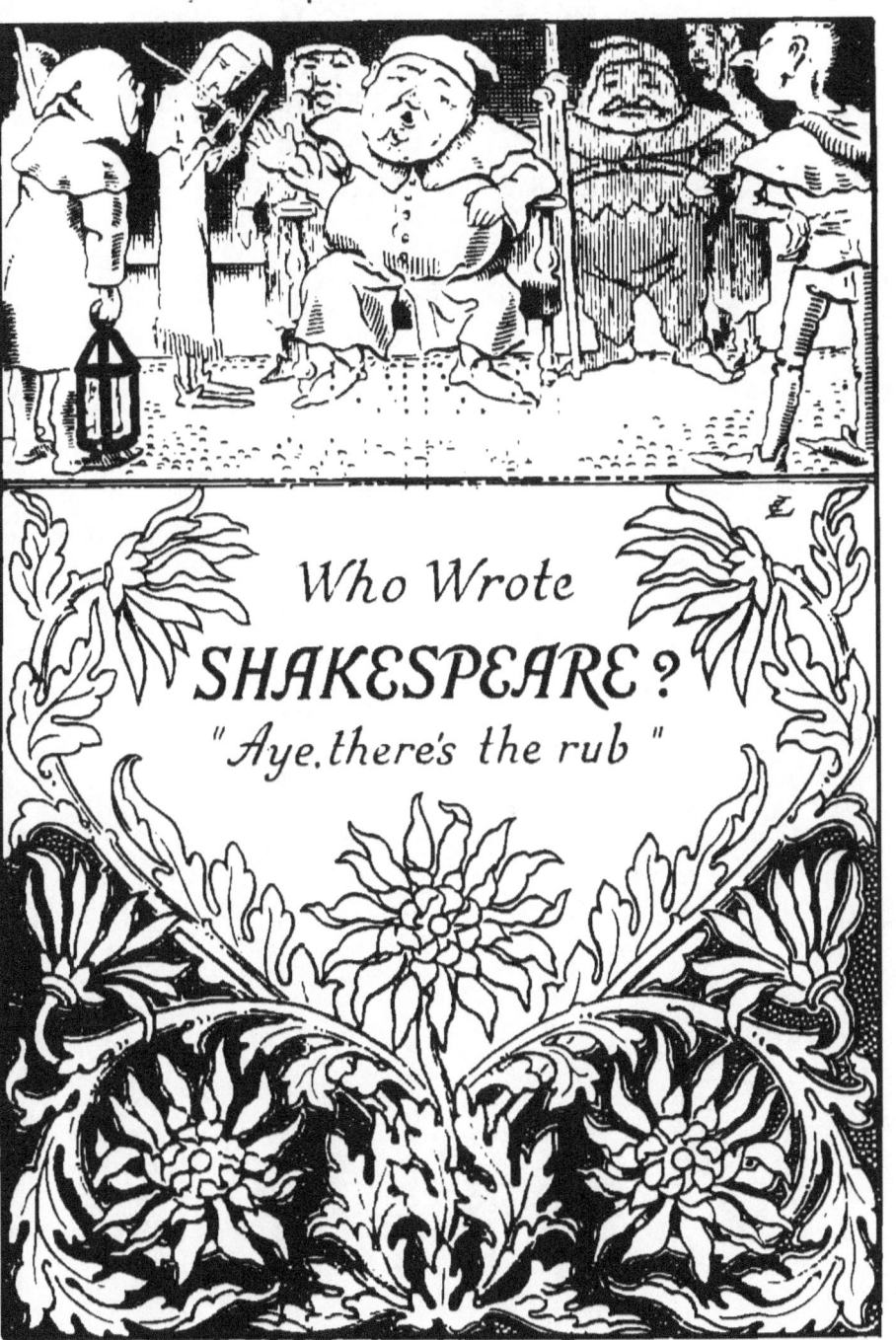

Who Wrote

SHAKESPEARE?

"Aye, there's the rub"

LONDON DAVID STOTT, 370, OXFORD STREET, W

DEDICATED, BY KIND PERMISSION, TO

HENRY IRVING, ESQ.

500 copies only of this edition have been printed.
of which 250 are ordered for America.

WHO WROTE "SHAKESPEARE"?

"Aye, there's the rub."

William Shakespeare

LINES ON THE PORTRAIT OF

Shakespeare

Prefixed as Frontispiece to the First Edition of
his Works in Folio, 1623.

To the Reader.

This figure, that thou here seest put,
It was for gentle Shakespeare cut;
Wherein the Grauer had a strife
With Nature, to out-doo the life:
O, could he but haue drawne his wit
As well in brasse, as he hath hit
His face; the Print would then surpasse
All, that was euer writ in brasse.
But, since he cannot, Reader, looke
Not on his Picture, but his Booke.

B. I.

"Who wrote Shakspere?" croaked a raven.

"Aye, who wrote 'Shakespeare'?—who but he
The world renowned!—from sea to sea,
From shore to shore—Bard of the Free—
            Sweet Avon's 'Will!'"

WHO WROTE SHAKESPEARE?

"Aye, there's the rub"

BY

WILLIAM HENDERSON

WITH PEN AND INK SKETCHES BY

CHARLES LYALL

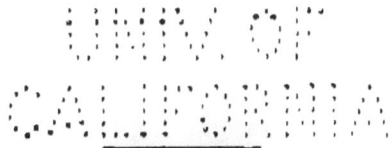

LONDON

DAVID STOTT, 370, OXFORD STREET, W

MDCCCLXXXVII

WHO WROTE "SHAKESPEARE"?

"Who wrote 'Shikspur'?"   "Boz!'
"Who the dickens is Boz?"
"Why, that *all of a twist* fellow!"

CANTER THE FIRST.

Dedicated to "The sect whose creed is 'honest doubt.'"

"Who wrote 'Shakspere'?" croaked a raven,
Perched upon the shrine of Avon :
Answering echoes rang, "'tis graven
　　　　　Here for evermore."

Mr. Faithful.

"Aye, who wrote 'Shakespeare'!—who but he
The world renowned !—from sea to sea,
From shore to shore—Bard of the Free—
　　　　　Sweet Avon's 'Will!'"

Mr. Doubtful.

" Nay, nay, my friend, thou art mistaken,
'Twas Lord Verul'am, known as Bacon !
He for the author now is taken
　　　　　Who wrote 'Shakspere.'"

Faith.

" *Who* wrote 'Shakespeare'? Say you Bacon ?
Leave of thy senses hast thou taken ?
Thou rasher of the rashest, waken !
　　　　　Nor idly dream.

" Deranged, good sir, must be thy mind !—
He who, though ' wisest, brightest shined,'
Was yet the ' meanest of mankind !'
　　　　　He write ' Shakespeare !'

" By J. O. H.-P.. F.R.S. !*
You've found a cipher, yet confess,
All ciphers are ye none the less
　　　　　Who've found out ' nowt.'"

---

* The noble efforts of Mr. J. O. Halliwell-Phillipps to preserve all that appertains to Avon's Bard, have earned for him the gratitude of the whole civilized world.

Nay, nay, my friend, thou art mistaken,
'Twas Lord Verul'am, known as Bacon '
He for the author now is taken
            Who wrote ' Shakspere.

Doubt.

" Stop, stop, good sir, not quite so fast,
We know !—we're learnèd, and can cast
Much light upon the tangled past,
         The ' Shakspear' skein."

" ' All negative our proof !' Quite so !
Hence it is difficult to show
This showman up, who seemed to know
         More than a Bacon :

" For Bacon's prose, we must admit,
Is not quite like what Shakspare writ,
Nor can we say Baconian wit
         Was like to his :

" All that we freely would admit,
In solemn judgment when we sit ;
But where is *your* proof ? not a bit
         Is positive !

" Aye, who wrote 'Shakspere' ? there's the rub :
Was't he who oft in Falcon ' pub '
With common sots would drink and grub,
                    Or play at ' Shovel ' ?

" Then fall at eve, 'neath crab-tree's shade,
In search of gravity, 'tis said,
Or crabs—no matter !—and there stayed
                    Till cocks did crow :

" Was't he who trespassed after deer
In Lucy's park of Charlcote near ?
And bridles held, when forced to steer
                    For London town ?

" Was't he whose Latin was but ' small ? '
Whose Greek was ' less,' or none at all ?
Had he the wit to crib or scrawl
                    What ' Shakspere ' writ ?

" The Grammar School was one in common
For son of butcher, son of yeoman ;
Who'll prove this 'greenhorn,' poacher, showman,
   Was there at all ?

" The English boy, with sharpest tool,
Must cut his name on board at school,
To prove that he is learned—no fool,
   But man of letters !

" Now where did ' Will,' at Grammar School,
Cut name on board, or desk, or stool,
To prove that he was not a fool ?—
   It can't be shown ! "

FAITH.

" Pooh ! any fool can cut his name !
Our Shakespeare *made his mark*, earned fame,
And left us an Immortal Name
   Carved on the Globe !

" ' What's in a name ? '—why, ' nowt ' to those
Vain carpers who as wise men pose :
Much learning makes them mad !—o'erthrows
                    What sense they had.

" ' What's in a name ? '—the English tongue
Was born again when Shakespeare sung !
The world has with the praises rung
                    Of Avon's Bard ! "

DOUBT.

" What say you ?   ' Robbie Burns got fou,
With Tam O' Shanter and such crew :
In taverns oft would toddy brew,
                    Till hours grew late ! '

" And that ' the learnèd " Sam " wrote plays,
Yet oft did grunt the tavern's praise—
With poets, wits, there spent his days,
                    Nor deemed it low ! '

The English boy, with sharpest tool,
Must cut his name on board at school,
To prove that he is learned—no fool,
                    But man of letters!

'Now where did 'Will' at Grammar School
Cut name on board, or desk, or stool,
To prove that he was not a fool ?—
                    It can't be shown !'

" But Robbie wrote not for the stage,
And Samuel, though prodigious sage,
Of prose and verse wrote many a page,
    Yet was no poet !"

FAITH.

" Sir Walter Scott wrote prose and verse ;
His works, 'tis needless to rehearse,
Have oft been played, and you can scarce
    Deny the fact."

DOUBT.

" True, but Sir Walter was no sot,
No patron he of ale-house pot :
The Mighty Minstrel was a Scot
    Who ne'er got fou ! "

FAITH.

" Pooh, pooh ! the bard, the Great Unknown,
At Ambrose's was right well known,
And yet that tavern since has grown
    A classic place !"

DOUBT.

" Of MS.—' copy '—not a bit
Exists to prove Shakespeare had wit
To write all that a ' Shakspere' writ :
If so where is 't ?

" 'Tis proved he could not write his name !
' Shake,' ' Shak,' ' spear,' 'spere'* were all the same
To this unlearnèd bore whom fame
Would rank as Bacon !

" Yet this is he for whom you claim
A world's applause—immortal fame !—
He really cannot be the same
Who wrote ' Shakspere ! '

---

* An industrious searcher has discovered forty-two different spellings of the name of the " Bard of Avon," as follows :—Chaesper, Schakespeire, Shackespeyre, Shackespear, Shackesper, Shackespere, Shackspear, Shackspeare, Shackspeer, Shacksper, Shackspere, Shackspire, Shagspere, Shakespear, Shakespeare, Shakespeere, Shakespere, Shakesphear, Shakespheare, Shakespurre, Shakispere, Shaksper, Shakspeare, Shakspeer, Shaksper, Shakspere, Shakspeyr, Shakspire, Shakysper, Shakyspere, Shaxbeer, Shaxber, Shaxberd, Shaxbere, Shaxespere, Shaxpeare, Shaxper, Shaxpere, Shaxspeare, Shenkspear, Shenkspeure, Shexpere.

" The thing 's absurd ! an actor rare
He might have been beyond compare ;
And yet, search where you will, is there
           A scrap of proof

" That he above Old Adam rose,
Or Hamlet's Ghost—such parts as those—
When he the buskin donned and hose
           On his own stage ?

" Who saw him born ? the where, the when,
Are all beyond our mortal ken :
The house, the room, the ' but,' the ' ben,'*
           Are mere conjecture !

" Who saw him born ? the day or night
Who'll prove, when first he saw the light :
No evidence have we the wight
           Was born at all !

—

* " A but and a ben " *(Scottice)*, the apartments of a two-roomed cottage.

" No proof have we that flea or fly
Ere jumped or flew who saw him die,
Give up the ghost, or pipe his eye,
                    When he did die !

" Who saw him die ? where's bedstead, bed,
The ' best,' on which was cut life's thread !
Were they consumèd as he sped
                    To unknown bourne ?

" The ' second-best ' he left, we know,
To Anne, his wife, his love to show !
But where and when—how did he go ?
                    We want to know.

" Mysterious all—birth, marriage, death,—
The ' curse '* left with his latest breath :
Whence came he ?—how left he this earth ?
                    Who can unfold ?

---

* "Good frend for Iesvs sake forbeare,
    To digg the dvst encloased henre :
    Bleste be the man that spares thes stones,
    And cvrst be he that moves my bones."

"Search where you will, is there
A scrap of proof

'That he above Old Adam rose,
Or Hamlet's Ghost--such parts as those--
When he the buskin donned and hose
On his own stage?"

" Had he, like Faust, a power at hand
Which no one human could withstand ?—
Wealth—knowledge—all ! at his command ?
                It might be so !

" Who knows ? perchance a cloven foot
He had !—no proof have we, to boot ;
A *tail* 'neath where he sat might shoot !—
                Played he the de'il ?"

FAITH.

Round Bacon nestles quite a litter
Of dryasdusts, the old, the bitter,
Each carping, crazy, critic critter
                For Bedlam fit.

They'll show you " parallels " absurd,
Concordance clear as milk in curd,
In *dictionary* every word
                That Shakespeare writ !

Oft are they pilgrims at the shrine
Of Bacon ? No ! Our " Bard Divine,"
They needs must gather still round thine
                At Avonside !

With all their theories and clatter,
Where Bacon lived and died ?—no matter!
The much loved name they would bespatter
    Is like a spell !

'Tis passing strange, they frequent stray
Where Avon sweetly wends its way !—
To Shakespeare and Anne Hathaway
    They still must cling !

Ye gods ! " what fools these mortals be ! "
At Shakespeare's shrine they bend the knee,
Yet vainly strive to prove that he
    Was but a fraud.

Let crack-brained pedants say their say,
His name, his works, will live for aye,
When croakers all have passed away
    To nameless graves.

The sect whose creed is " honest doubt,"
Tradition—all things sacred—scout !
They 'll prove that Shakespeare, without doubt,
    No mother had !

The doughty doubter *hath-a-way*
Of proving Anne was, lack-a-day !
Not Shakespeare's spouse, but other clay
          Than Shottery !

The doubter's epitaph should be :- -
" That *rare* sense—common sense—lacked he—
" His bonnet ever held a bee,
          Or a ' mare's nest ! ' "

He 'll prove that Shakespeare was a ghost,
Or clown, who ne'er could learning boast !
That, " all in all," he was at most
          A raw-chaw-Bacon !

He 'll prove that New Place was not old,
That Gastrell, shepherd of the fold,
Would an' he could a tale unfold !—
          He could, no doubt !

He 'll show foundations old and new :
The parson this, not that, o'erthrew—
Precisely !—that's just what we knew,
          He razed " ' *NEW* ' PLACE."

" Oh, not at all !" says Honest Doubt,
" All vain tradition we must scout,
" We 've found the old foundations out
                    Of Shakspare's home."

And yet it may be clearly shown
The venerable base of stone,
For ages hid and overgrown,
                    Proves the reverse.

Faith may presume, but yet would know
If Shakespeare, when he left " the show,"
Did to the *largest* mansion go
                    In Stratford Town ?

For so 'tis said.   But Doubt would trace
In smallest, oldest house, " *New* Place ! "
He 'll have to try and prove his case
                    Some other way.

UNIV. OF
CALIFORNIA

' all in all, he was at most
A raw-chaw-Bacon !'

It is not clear that old is new,
And that the smaller of the two
Was once the largest house " on view "
                    In Stratford Town.

But Doubt can show a builder's bill
To prove that *the great house* " of " Will "
Was by an earlier Vandal still
                    Than Francis razed.

It was much pulled about, we know,
But further light they'll have to throw
On these old stones before they show
                    Their proof is clear.

Of builder's bills we've seen a few—
Just let them *your* old house " renew,"
They'll say it is " as good as new "
                    When they have done !

New Place was possibly " restored "—
" Recovered " ! yet not lost nor " floored,"
Till Gastrell, Goth of Goths abhorred,
                    Demolished all.

When, through the ravages of time,
To ruin crumbles stone and lime,
Then " restoration " is no crime,
                    But watch it well.

'Twere better that our fanes decay
Through age, than be " improved " away :
For State protection let us pray,
                    To guard them all.

To dryasdusts we dare to say,
The parson was a bird of prey !
We find but skeletons to-day
                    Where he had been.

Evanishing 'mid ruin's rack,
He left no shadow on his track,
But Lyall dips his quill, and back
                    He comes anew !

The Rev. Francis Gastrell,

*Who, "**sans eyes, sans taste, sans everything,**" cut down Shakespeare's celebrated mulberry tree, "because he was so pestered with visitors!" and levelled the house to the ground at "New Place," in which the poet is reputed to have lived and died, "because it was rated too high!"*

WHO WAS THE VANDAL?

CANTER THE SECOND.

A kind of Highland fling—"Lay on, Macduff!"—that sort of thing.

———◆———

Alas, poor Vandal! who can find
One shred of beauty in thy mind?
Thou wert at feud with all mankind—
    Ill deeds were thine.

No "touch of nature" made thee "kin"
With aught of goodness—aught but sin:
There surely dwelt thy soul within
    A master fiend.

From age to age thy hateful name,
Linked with the Swan of Avon's fame,
Unmatched shall be for deeds of shame!—
    Why wert thou born?

I would not over-rate the least
This parasite in shape of—priest,
Who fled, pursued by man and beast,
    To save his neck.

A *cursory* remark I'd make,
That Francis well deserved the stake.
For all the havoc he did make
                    In Stratford town.

But let us fairly state the case,
To rate him high was a disgrace !
For he was low, and set his face
                    'Gainst all things high.

In lines " vnpolisht " I'd unfold
The parson's tale, and how he " sold "
The very souls whose cure, we 're told,
                    He undertook.

Like Bottom, Gastrell was " translated,"
By rustics he was rusticated,
And all through being over-rated !
                    Alas, poor cure !

The simple facts traditions tell,
The house he cleared, the tree did fell,
But saved his trunk, then went to—well !
                    They don't say where.

" ' Something attempted, something done.
This Ostrogoth for life did run,
'A name to live' had he not won ?
                    Why should he die ?'"

He reasoned thus, "The mulb'ry tree
" Brings countless visitors to me !
" It thus offends, and why should ' we '
            " Not cut it down ?

" Are we not taught in Holy Writ
" If aught offend, it is not fit
" That it should live" ?   And in a fit
            He cut it down !

The tree, the house, were his, we 're told !
Aye, they were his to guard and hold,
As priceless treasures—countless gold !
            Not to destroy !

Irreverent, ill-conditioned hound,
Who razed our bard's house to the ground,
Should thy sepulchral hole be found,
            It *may* be cursed !

A hound ! good dog, we pardon crave,
Thou 'rt ever faithful, ever brave :
No " reverend " thou, yet oft would save
            Thy trust, or die !

The Poet's malison on thee
Who cut down Shakespeare's mulb'ry tree!
More trees there were for such as thee
          To hang thyself!

If cursed be he the *bones* who'd touch,
Of Avon's Bard, in Stratford Church,
Did he not leave his *baneful* touch
          On house and tree?

Pray, gentle reader, be not shocked!
For less, priests oft have been unfrocked!
For less, oft at a rope's end rocked,
          Or " rode the stang."

The parson searched for "tongues in trees,"
" Sermons in stones " !—not finding these,
His flock grew weary—ill at ease,
          When he did preach.

Would that he first had searched for " books
In" Warwick's many " running brooks " !
And found in one of Avon's nooks
          A cool retreat.

" *The Poet's malison on thee*
Who cut down Shakespeare's mulb'ry tree
More trees there were for such as thee
To hang thyself!"

Too late, the village Hampdens came
To stay this Vandal's deed of shame :
The work was done, and Gastrell's fame
            Made infamous !

To save his bacon and his gown,
He fled, pursued by dog and clown :
In infamy he sought renown,
            Nor sought in vain.

Like him of Ephesus renown,
Who burnt Diana's Temple down,
What cared the parson for the town ?
            'Twas fame he sought !

" Something attempted, something done,"
This Ostrogoth for life did run,
" A name to live " had he not won !
            Why should he die ?

He would not seek a martyr's crown,
Enough he'd done to gain renown !
" Shure," all the trees were not cut down !
            And " rope was cheap ! "

Well didst thou take thyself away,
Nor dare dishonour Stratford clay :
Unhallowed was thy natal day,
    Unblest thy last !

No mulb'ry tree will cast its shade
Where thy dishonoured bones are laid ;
Scarce on thy grave a grassy blade
    Will raise its head !

Thy bones God's-acre could not hold,
They'd turn and flee the sacred mould ;
Another place, not quite so cold,
    Was fit for thee.

Alas ! poor Very Rev. Gastrell !
Thy thick skull now is known too well ;
No Hamlet thy good deeds can tell,
    Unloved art thou !

Another guy let Stratford boast,
His effigy, like Guy Fawkes, roast !
When yearly ye the memory toast—
    " Sweet Avon's Bard."

To Mr. Richard Savage,

(Secretary and Librarian, Shakespeare's birthplace, Stratford-on-Avon.)

𝕾𝔀𝔢𝔢𝔱 𝔄𝔳𝔬𝔫𝔰𝔦𝔡𝔢!

(By W. Henderson, on first visiting Stratford, August 2, 1886.)

Sweet Avonside! to nations dear,
Who dwell afar from England here,
Age after age may come and go,
As Avon's waters gently flow,
But graven deeper will the name
Of Shakespeare be on scroll of fame!
From distant and more distant lands
Now press the steps of pilgrim bands,
And all mankind, the wide world o'er,
With rapture turn to Britain's shore:
For this, our sea-girt isle, is named
As Freedom's home—for Shakespeare famed!
Where'er the feet of freemen tread
There will our poet's verse be read,

Where Freedom shakes off every yoke—
Where'er the English tongue is spoke!
Nay! Foreign tongues—all lands will tell—
'Twas here the Immortal Bard did dwell!
Here first he breathed, lived, loved, and came
To die, but deathless is his fame!
Prophetic name!—*The Globe*, thy stage :
Bard of All Time!—in every age
The world will glory in thy page!

LONDON : HENDERSON, RAIT, & SPALDING, PRINTERS, 3 & 5, MARYLEBONE LANE, W.

www.ingramcontent.com/pod-product-compliance
Lightning Source LLC
Chambersburg PA
CBHW030903260626
47169CB00008B/2665